MY ROOTS ARE RICH

Written By
Nyla Choates

Illustrated By
Whimsical Designs By CJ

About The Author

Meet the Author **Nyla Choates!** She is an 18-year-old youth activist and Freshman at Spelman College from Milpitas, California. Nyla has a passion for empowering, inspiring, and educating people as well as fighting systemic racism within the educational system. Nyla's favorite quote is, "You have to be the change that you want to see in the world." She wants to be the change. She hopes you enjoy her first book, as this story is based on her personal experience as a young girl.

This book is dedicated to my beautiful, loving parents.
Thank you both for instilling in me that my roots are rich.

It's the first day of school! I can't wait to go.
To meet some new friends and learn as I grow!

I put on my shoes and I rush out the door.
I may be nervous but I have lots to explore!

As I walk into class and look all around,
I wonder why no one that looks
like me can be found?

We open our books and to my surprise,
there still is no one that looks like me that's inside.

Everyone else has people that look just like them.
But what about me? Where do I stem?

I put my head down, and my face started to frown.
I think to myself, why can't i be rich,
and grow from the ground?

The dirt that I sow must be nothing but dead.
Or is it the dirt that I sow, was taught to my head?

I think to myself, am I a diamond?
a precious gem?

Well, how will I know when I am not fed?

As I put my head up and look to the sky,
a voice from within is heard from inside.

Saying, **your roots are rich!**
And they are older than time!

And your knowledge of self,
they grow through the vines.

The vines and the veins
grow within your skin.

The vines and the veins come from that seed that is within.

The vines and the veins are what form you inside.

The vines and the veins are what make you divine!

Deep in the soil, you are rooted in love.

Deep in the soil,
you are from the ancestors above.

You are more precious than diamonds....

...more valuable than gold.

You are a descendant of queens...

Now that i know where my roots are from,
I can't wait to tell the world...